What a day. Blast Off Boy sure was exhausted from all that silly hoopla over being chosen to participate in the Galactic Space Exchange Program. Johnny Smith, dubbed "Blast Off Boy" by his hometown newspaper, had been chosen out of millions as the most average kid on the planet. He was being sent to represent Earth on the newly discovered planet of Meep. An alien family would take him into their home, and he would attend the local school. He was starting to wish that the whole thing was over already.

On planet Meep, a little green alien boy named Blorp Glorp was also making plans. He was on his way to Earth. He would be staying with the Smith family and going to the Davis Elementary School. Blorp loved adventures. He simply couldn't wait for this one to begin.

for Robert

Visit hyperionchildrensbooks.com
First Edition
1 3 5 7 9 10 8 6 4 2
Printed in Singapore

Library   of   Congress   Cataloging-in-Publication   Data
Yaccarino, Dan.   First day on a strange new planet / Dan
Yaccarino. —1st ed. p. cm. — (Blast Off Boy and Blorp;)
Summary: Two elementary students, one from Earth and one
from the newly discovered planet Meep, exchange places.
ISBN 0-7868-0578-1 (trade). — ISBN 0-7868-2499-9 (lib.)
[1. Student exchange programs—Fiction   2. Life on other
planets—Fiction   3. Schools—Fiction]   I. Title   II. Series:
Yaccarino, Dan. Blast Off Boy and Blorp; I.   PZ7.Y125Fi 2000
[E]—dc21   99-39772   CIP

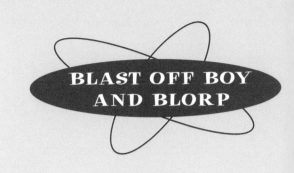

BLAST OFF BOY
AND BLORP

First Day on a Strange New Planet

written and illustrated by
DAN YACCARINO

Hyperion Books for Children
New York

Blast Off Boy was more than a little nervous. First, he had just met the family he would be staying with on planet Meep: Mr. and Mrs. Glorp and their daughter, Blippy. Second, it was the first day of Galactic Grammar School.

"And now I have to find a seat on the big yellow space bus. Uggh," he said.

"Swell, the only free seat is next to a kid with two heads. Gross."

As the bus zoomed along, the other kids laughed and talked about their summer vacations floating in the Milky Way and touring the moons of Jupiter. Blast Off Boy stared out the window, watching the stars fly by.

"Hi! My name is Buzzopod," said one head.

"And my name is Bozopod," said the other.

"But you can call us Buzz and Bo," the two heads said together.

"Uh, hi," said Blast Off Boy, still looking out the window.

Blast Off Boy wished he was back in his old school, back on his old planet, good old Earth. He knew everybody there. The kids are weird and strange here, he thought. This stinks.

Meanwhile, back on good old Earth, Blorp could hardly contain himself. He had just met his new family, Mr. and Mrs. Smith, their son, Lenny, and their dog, Scooter.

"I'm looking forward to my first day at Davis Elementary," he said. "You know, I've never been anywhere outside my solar system before!"

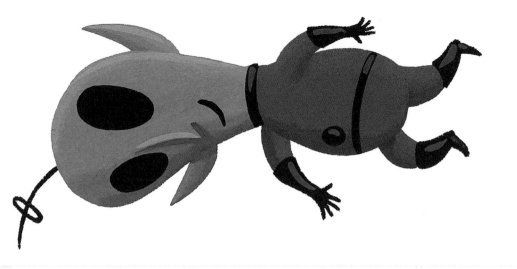

In homeroom, Blorp was so excited, he kept floating up to the ceiling.

"Please take your seat, Blorp," said Ms. Jacobs.

The other students quietly moved their desks away from him. Blorp didn't notice, and he wouldn't have cared anyway. He was in a new school on a new planet, and he was happy.

Blast Off Boy looked at his schedule. *Advanced nuclear calculus,* it read. "Oh no!" he said. "We haven't covered that yet in school." He sat behind the biggest kid he could find so he wouldn't be called on. He didn't realize she was transparent until it was too late.

"Blast Off Boy—yes, you. Would you tell us the square root of .769FQ87$\frac{1}{2}$?" said Miss Hologram.

Nuts, the first question in my first class on the first day in a new school and my mind is blank! he thought.

Blast Off Boy nervously looked around the room. All 67 eyes were on him. He looked at the bottom of his space boot and blurted out, "4$\frac{1}{2}$ B?"

"Correct!" beamed Miss Hologram.

It's a good thing he had big feet.

The chemistry class was frightened as Blorp mixed chemicals together that made strange colors and mysterious smells. They were downright petrified when a big blue mushroom grew from a test tube. Everyone watched wide-eyed as he poured twenty different chemicals into a beaker and shook them up.

They gasped as he gulped it down. The
room started to shake.

When they looked up, Blorp was so big, his head touched the ceiling.

"Blorp, get down here immediately!"
Mrs. Pomerantz hollered.

Blorp got a week's detention.

It was lunchtime on planet Meep. "Help! Help!" cried Blast Off Boy as he ran out of the cafeteria. "There's a monster in there!"

"Where?" asked Buzz.

"I don't see anything," said Bo.

"There!" Blast Off Boy pointed. A big purple blob with one eye was oozing through the doorway.

"Oh, that," Buzz said.

"That's just the lunch special," said Bo. "I'd stay away from it, too."

Blast Off Boy didn't quite feel like eating after that, so he just took a seat in the back of the lunch orb by himself.

But the weird kid with the two heads followed him and sat down next to him.

Oh, great, thought Blast Off Boy. This gross-looking kid is bothering me again.

Gee, I wish I were back at my old school right now. Today is fish sticks and green Jell-O day.

"Our mom made us a photon and jelly sandwich with the crusts cut off," Bo said. "You want half?"

Blast Off Boy looked at it floating there. It was no fish stick, that's for sure, but he *was* kind of hungry.

It wasn't that bad, actually. Mom's meat loaf wasn't much better.

In the lunchroom at Davis Elementary, Blorp opened his lunch storage unit. "Yeeecccchhh!" Katy said. A small purple blob oozed out of it. Its one eye blinked and looked around.

"Oh, boy!" cried Blorp. "Titanium Tetrazzini! You want some?"

Katy could only answer "Ulp," as she covered her mouth and ran off to the girls' room.

"Okay! More for me!" Blorp said, slurping it up.

The other kids moved to another table.

"That stuff is gross! How can you *eat* it?" Jimmy hollered.

"What's that green stuff *you're* eating?" asked Blorp.

"Jell-O," said Jimmy, as he slurped it up.

Blast Off Boy's day wasn't getting any better. In quantum chemistry class, he tried his best to hide, but he was called on anyway.

In galactic gym class he got hit in the head with a sport sphere.

In advanced molecular biology class, he realized the zipper on his space suit was down. Who knew how long he'd been walking around like that?

Then, on his way to his last class, Blast Off Boy got so lost he had no idea where he was. "Why do things like this happen to me?" he sighed.

Blorp's biology teacher, Mr. Schwartz, broke some bad news to the children about the class hamster.

"Leon is very ill," Mr. Schwartz said. "He won't eat or run on his little wheel. I'm afraid I don't know what's wrong."

"May I see him?" Blorp asked the teacher.

Mr. Schwartz handed Leon to Blorp. The hamster began to glow.

The horrified class screamed and shouted.

"He's gonna eat Leon!" Katy cried.

"Eat him?" Blorp said. "I was just making him better. I would never eat your hamster. I'm allergic to them."

Blorp placed Leon back in his cage. Leon blinked his eyes, wiggled his nose, and jumped onto his little wheel. "He's well again," cried Katy. The class cheered.

Blorp got extra credit.

Maybe, the class thought, this new kid is not so bad after all.

Blast Off Boy made a wrong turn down a wrong hallway, which led to a dead end.

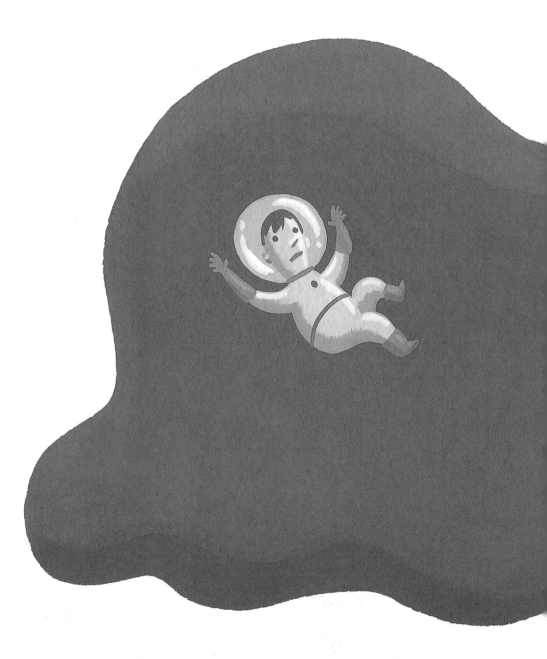

When he turned around, there it was. Big
and purple with one huge eye hungrily staring
at him: the lunch special.

Blast Off Boy yelled as the purple ooze
swallowed him up.

Through the purple ooze, Blast Off Boy heard
a shout.

"Cough him up, you crummy leftover!" cried
Buzz and Bo as they whacked the lunch special

with an advanced molecular biology textbook.

The lunch special spat out Blast Off Boy and slithered back to the cafeteria.

Blast Off Boy sat in a puddle of purple slime, not quite sure what had happened.

"Gee, thanks," he said. "I could've been tomorrow's lunch special."

"No problem," said Buzz.

"So, you wanna play scudball after school today?" asked Bo.

"Sure." Blast Off Boy smiled as he scraped off the purple crud. "Let's go!"

Looking back on everything that had happened that day, Blast Off Boy thought, Maybe this new place is not so bad after all.